To N and C and K and C,
for all the love you've given me.
-AH

For dedicated Dads everywhere.
-AC

🐝 little bee books

A division of Bonnier Publishing
853 Broadway, New York, New York 10003
Text copyright © 2016 by Alastair Heim
Illustrations copyright © 2016 by Alisa Coburn
LITTLE BEE BOOKS is a trademark of Bonnier Publishing Group, and associated
colophon is a trademark of Bonnier Publishing Group.
Manufactured in China   LEO 0716
First Edition   10 9 8 7 6 5 4 3 2 1
ISBN 978-1-4998-0174-3

littlebeebooks.com
bonnierpublishing.com

Library of Congress Cataloging-in-Publication Data:
Names: Heim, Alastair, author. | Coburn, Alisa, illustrator.
Title: Love You Too / by Alastair Heim ; illustrated by Alisa Coburn.
Description: New York : Little Bee Books, 2016. | Summary: Follows a father and child through a busy day as
they play a rhythmic game of call-and-response, starting and ending with "When I say I love, you say you."
Identifiers: LCCN 2015049672 | ISBN 9781499801743 (hardback)
Subjects: | CYAC: Fathers and daughters—Fiction. | Pigs—Fiction. | BISAC: JUVENILE FICTION /
Family / Parents. | JUVENILE FICTION / Animals / Pigs. | JUVENILE FICTION / Love & Romance.
Classification: LCC PZ7.1.H4448 Lov 2016 | DDC [E]—dc23
LC record available at https://lccn.loc.gov/2015049672

Love You Too

Too

by Alastair Heim   illustrated by Alisa Coburn

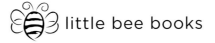 little bee books

When I say "I love,"
you say "you."

When I say "love you,"
you say "too."

When I say "time to,"
you say "dress."

When I say "this one,"
you say "yes."

When I say "pancakes,"
you say "more."

When I say "syrup,"
you say "pour."

When I say "ready,"
you say "go."

When I say "slower,"
you say "no."

When I say "swing me,"
you say "high."

When I say "let's have," you say "lunch."

Both of us go *crunch, crunch, crunch.*

When I say "in the,"
you say "tub."

When I say "scrub-a-,"
you say "dub."

When I say "jammies,"
you say "please."

When I say "which book,"
you say "these."

When I say "time for,"
you say "bed."

When I say "sleepy-,"
you say "head."

When I say "hug me,"
you say "tight."

When I say "night-y," you say "night."

When I say "I love,"
you say "you."

When I say "love you,"
you say "too."